Where Do Fairies Go When It Snows?

Liza Gardner Walsh

Illustrated by Hazel Mitchell

Down East Books
Camden, Maine

To my children, for all the questions
—L. G. W.

To Trish, who is always in fairyland
—H. M.

Published by Down East Books
An imprint of The Rowman & Littlefield Publishing Group, Inc.
4501 Forbes Boulevard, Suite 200, Lanham, Maryland 20706
www.rowman.com

Unit A, Whitacre Mews, 26-34 Stannary Street, London SE11 4AB, United Kingdom

Distributed by NATIONAL BOOK NETWORK

British Library Cataloguing in Publication Information Available

Library of Congress Cataloging-in-Publication Data
Library of Congress Cataloging-in-Publication Data Available
ISBN 978-1-60893-413-3 (cloth : alk. paper) — ISBN 978-1-60893-414-0 (electronic)

The paper used in this publication meets the minimum requirements of American National Standard for Information Sciences—Permanence of Paper for Printed Library Materials, ANSI/NISO Z39.48-1992.

Printed in the United States of America
Manufactured by Thomson-Shore, Dexter, MI (USA); RMA81HS02, September, 2015

Do fairies hibernate like bears,
hedgehogs, and raccoons,
or are they like squirrels collecting
food under the winter moon?

Do they rely on the flowers and sunshine of spring
to make the magic of their fairy world sing?

BUT when the days get cold, dark, and dreary,
do their spirits get low and do they feel weary?

AFTER a busy summer of parties and visiting fairy towns,

do they rest their drowsy heads and put their fairy dust down?

Do they curl under leafy blankets
or beneath mushroom caps,
placing fragile wings on moss
for a long winter nap?

ARE they resting in *your* fairy house,
hiding under snow,
its fairy door sealed tight
against frosty winds that blow?

ARE they tucked in
with magical dreams in their heads,
nestled 'neath feathers and grass
in a sea shell bed?

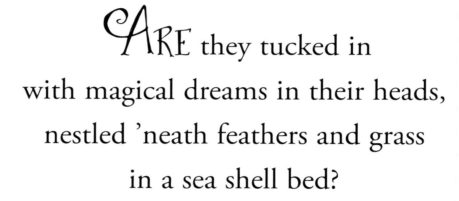

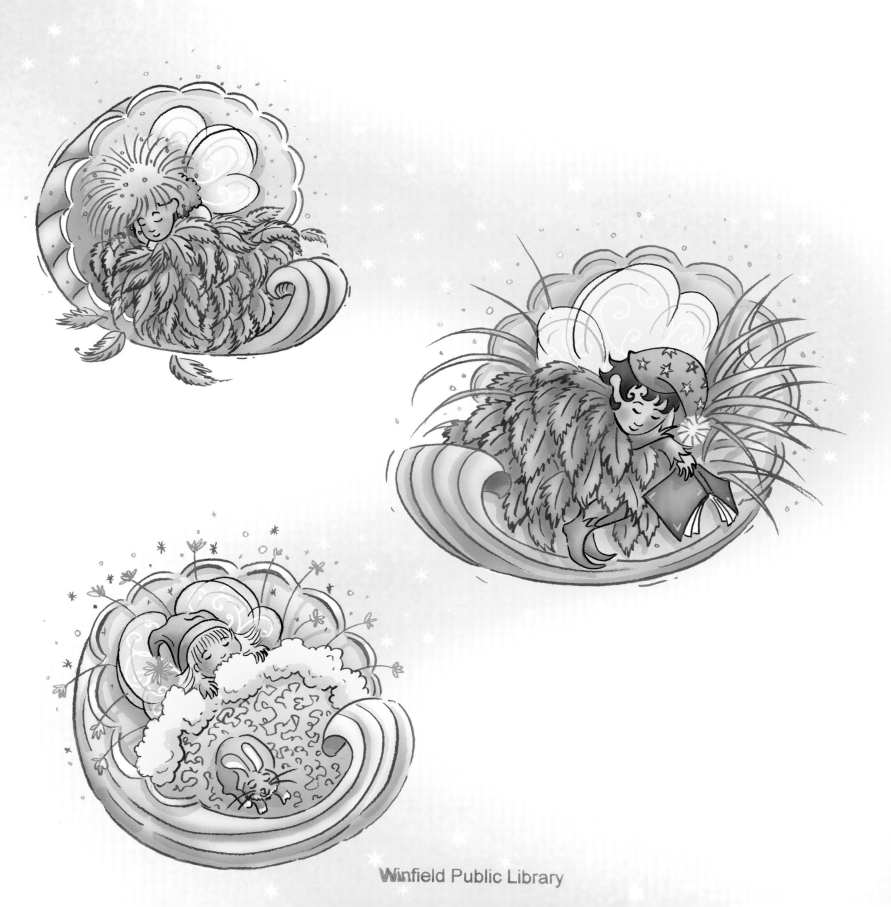

DO they make little jackets
of downy milkweed
and knit hats and mittens
from feathery reeds?

AND in this winter finery,
do they dance by firelight,
gathering in the storm to
warm up the freezing night?

DO they help the birds and animals get settled,
finding leftover berries, acorn caps, and dried nettles?

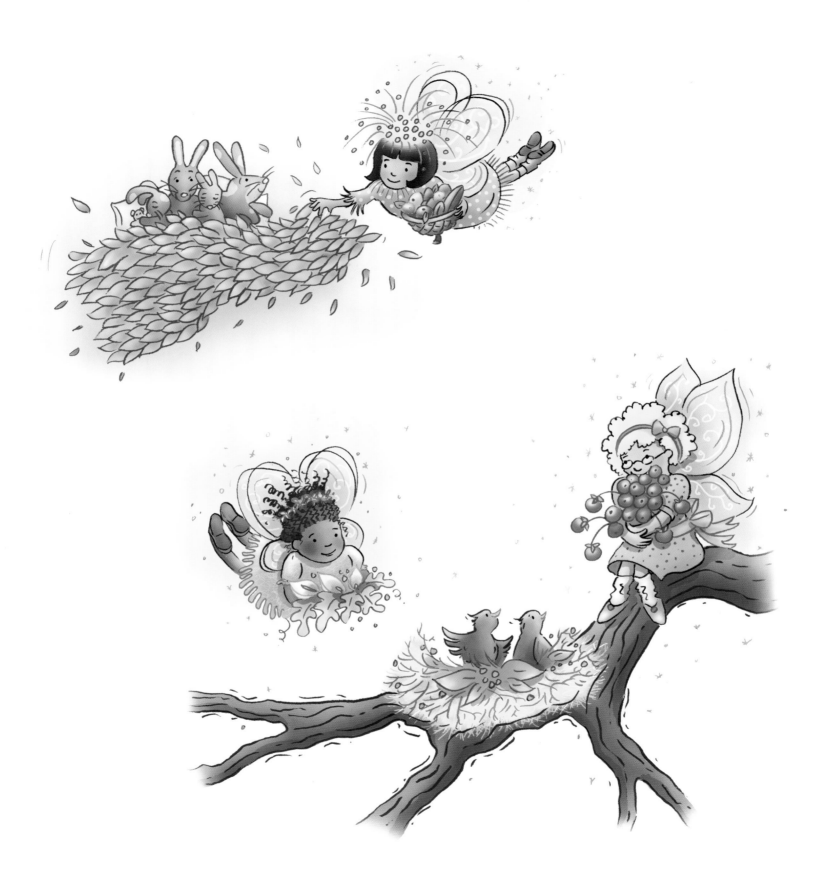

WITH all of this gathering,
do they have a big feast,
where they imagine summer
and its gentle heat?

Do fairies hibernate, oh, do you know?
Have they whispered their secrets of where they go?

PERHAPS to be safe,
in case they're hovering close,
leave out a tiny pancake, some milk,
or a crumble of toast.

MAKE a winter house for these fairies in need,
build a roof, four walls, and add a sprinkle of seed.

GATHER some twigs, bark, and pine cones,

for you never know if a fairy is shivering alone.

FOR this is the same kindness that fairies show you.
Helping each other is what we all should do.

And when spring returns with its green and growing things,

keep a sharp eye out to see what the fairies bring.

Ways You Can Take Care of Fairies in the Winter

During the cold months, one way to warm a fairy's heart is to provide them with a winter snack. Leaving small bowls of milk and honey is one way to keep the fairies happy, or you can make dried fruit and seed garlands to string on trees. Similar to stringing garlands for a Christmas tree, a fairy garland requires a needle and thread. Popcorn, cranberries, slices of oranges and apples, as well as walnuts can all be strung together for the fairies to snack on through the cold months. You can also take bread and use cookie cutters to cut out shapes. Slather these shapes with peanut butter or margarine and dip into birdseed. These can be strung on the garland or on their own to attract a variety of the fairies' winged friends.